DUDLEY SCHOOLS LIBRARY
AND INFORMATION SERVICE

Sound

KU-394-283

Schools Library and Information Services

S00000682310

DUDLEY P

L - 47 992

682310   SOH

JYIRV

First published in Great Britain in 2005 by Bloomsbury Publishing Plc
38 Soho Square, London, W1D 3HB

Text copyright © Garp Enterprises Ltd 1998, 2003
Illustrations copyright © Tatjana Hauptmann 2003/Diogenes Verlag AG Zurich
The moral rights of the author and illustrator have been asserted

All rights reserved
No part of this publication may be reproduced or
transmitted by any means, electronic, mechanical, photocopying
or otherwise, without the prior permission of the publisher

A CIP catalogue record of this book is available from the British Library
ISBN 0 7475 7293 3

Printed and bound in China by C & C Offset Printing Co., Ltd.

1 3 5 7 9 10 8 6 4 2

All papers used by Bloomsbury Publishing are natural, recyclable products made from wood grown in well-managed forests.
The manufacturing processes conform to the environmental regulations of the country of origin.

A Sound
Like Someone
Trying Not
to Make a Sound

A Story by
John Irving
Illustrated by
Tatjana Hauptmann

BLOOMSBURY
CHILDREN'S
BOOKS

Tom woke up, but Tim did not. It was the middle of the night.

'Did you hear that?'
Tom asked his brother.

9

But Tim was only two.
Even when he was awake, he didn't talk much.

Tom woke up his
father and asked him:
'Did you hear
that sound?'

13

'What did it sound like?' his father asked.

'It sounded like a monster with no arms and no legs, but it was trying to move,' Tom said.

'How could it move with no arms and legs?' his father asked.

'It wriggles,' Tom said. 'It slides on its fur.'

'Oh, it has fur?' his father asked.

'It pulls itself along with its teeth,' Tom said.

'It has teeth, too!' his father exclaimed.

'I told you – it's a monster!' Tom said.

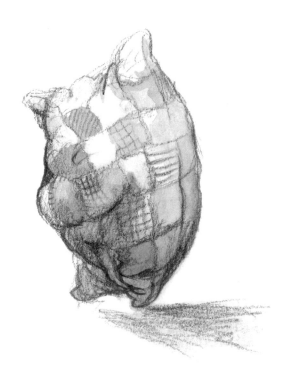

'But what exactly was the sound that woke you up?' his father asked.

'It was a sound like, in the closet, if one of Mummy's dresses came alive and it tried to climb down off the hanger,' Tom said.

20

'Let's go back to your room and listen for the sound,' Tom's father said.

And there was Tim, still asleep – he still hadn't heard the sound.

It was a sound like someone pulling the nails out of the floorboards under the bed. It was a sound like a dog trying to open a door. Its mouth was wet, so it couldn't get a good grip on the doorknob, but it wouldn't stop trying – eventually the dog would get in, Tom thought.

It was a sound like a ghost in the attic, dropping the peanuts it had stolen from the kitchen.

It was a sound like someone trying not to make a sound.

'There's the sound again!' Tom whispered to his father. 'Did you hear that?'

This time, Tim woke up, too. It was a sound like something caught inside the headboard of the bed. It was eating its way out – it was gnawing through the wood.

It seemed to Tom that the sound was definitely the sound of an armless, legless monster dragging its thick, wet fur.

'It's a monster!' Tom cried.

'It's just a mouse crawling between the walls,' his father said.

Tim screamed. He didn't know what a "mouse" was. It frightened him to think of something with wet, thick fur – and no arms and no legs – crawling between the walls. How did something like that get between the walls, anyway?

But Tom asked his father, 'It's just a mouse?'

His father thumped against the wall with his hand and they listened to the mouse scurrying away. 'If it comes back again,' he said to Tom and Tim, 'just hit the wall.'

'A mouse crawling between the walls!' said Tom. 'That's all it was!'

He quickly fell asleep, and his father went back to bed
and fell asleep, too, but Tim was awake the whole night long,
because he didn't know what a mouse was and he wanted
to be awake when the thing crawling between the walls
came crawling back.

Each time he thought he heard the mouse crawling between
the walls, Tim hit the wall with his hand and the mouse
scurried away – dragging its thick, wet fur and its no arms
and legs with it.

And that is the end of the story.

JOHN IRVING, born in Exeter, New Hampshire, in 1942, lives in southern Vermont. In a badly heated room in Vienna he wrote the first of meanwhile ten novels, *Setting Free the Bears*. Fame came with his fourth book, *The World According to Garp*, after which all of his following novels (s. a. *The Hotel New Hampshire*, *A Prayer for Owen Meany*, *A Widow for One Year*, *The Fourth Hand*) became world best sellers. For the screenplay of *The Cider House Rules* he even got an Oscar in 2000.

TATJANA HAUPTMANN, born in Wiesbaden (Germany) in 1950, became known through her first children's book *Ein Tag im Leben der Dorothea Wutz* (A Day in the Life of Dorothea Wutz) and as an illustrator of *Das große Märchenbuch* (The Big Book of Fairytales). Her breakthrough came in 2002 with an illustrated edition of Mark Twain's *Die Abenteuer von Tom Sawyer und Huckleberry Finn* (The Adventures of Tom Sawyer and Huckleberry Finn). Tatjana Hauptmann lives near Zurich.